USA TODAY BEST SELLING AUTHOR

DANIEL ARTHUR SMITH

GAZER

First Edition

Special thanks to Jessica West

ISBN-13: 978-1946777478 ISBN-10: 1946777471

Cover By Daniel Arthur Smith

~*~

For Susan, Tristan, & Oliver, as all things are.

~*~

GAZER

Daniel Arthur Smith
Edited for Narration by Jessica West

~*~

THEY CALL IT GAZIN, tha way ya lock eyes onta one of tha tall lizard birds, make 'em freeze solid, stare back inta ya. I was really good at it, say so mahself. Best in Ms. Tilly's third grade fa sure, best on Mars maybe, cept Daddy of course.

"Ginny? How ya stare so long," little Bill would always ask. He was little then anyway. mah baby brotha, jess as high as that red concrete wall still runs tha side tha road from mah Daddy's farm ta Perta.

It's been years past, but I remember tha day.

I was gazin at one of tha big hens—Jessy. She's a three-meter lizard, an Imperial Strider—twice mah height easy. Tha Imperials are so beautiful, with tha way their purple and blue foe feathers flow off their arms, and tha way tha light ripples across tha soft fuchsia bands around

1

their necks, and those long fluffy blue feathery tails—gorgeous creatures.

And I remember it was a warmer day, cuz there was a sweet breeze comin across tha field where we keep tha birds, blowin clear from tha reservoir. Ya could smell tha yella honey suckle rose that grew in bunches on tha shore. Little Bill was whisperin low and quiet like down by mah side. His tiny fingers were hooked inta tha metal chain link so he could jess peek over tha edge of that red concrete that made up tha bottom half of tha fence.

"It's not hard a'tall," I told 'em, and I remember mah mouth was barely movin cuz I was standin statue like, mah glare fixed on tha big ole blue saucer of an eye in tha center of that bird's head.

"Ain't ya scared?" he asked.

"Scareda what?" I asked back.

"Scared that old bird'll git inta yer head," he said. "That's what Helen told me can happen. Git right in there, read yer thoughts, and fry yer pan. 'Specially if they raise tha crown feathers."

Helen was a girl from his playgroup. She was always messin with little Bill. "Ya need ta stop lissenin ta her. Jessy here ain even got no crown feathers anyhow."

"Ya she does."

"No, those plumes is a crest, that's not tha same thing. Her feathers are longer than tha otha striders, but that's only cuz she's an Imperial. Only racers and breeders have proppa crowns, ya know that sho nuff. Ole Benny's tha only one with bouncin feathers on his cap round here, one, cuz he's a firetail and two, tha only breeder Daddy's allowed ta have. But he's dumb as a moon rock, so he ain fryin nobody's pan no how. Ya know Daddy had ta pull him outta Shadow Canyon again, cuz tha dead end walls confused tha dumb ole bird? Again. Dumb as a moon rock."

Little Bill ducked down ta hide himself behind tha short red wall. "Well, this one gives me tha creepers."

I didn care much what mah little brotha had ta say about that in particular. I took it as a matter of pride ta lock that bird inta place. Jessy'd been scratchin tha sand when little Bill and I came along and she would've sprint off if it was anyone one else. But not from me, oh no. All I had ta do was stiffen up, lock on, and BAM! She was mine.

Daddy said it was a gift.

I was real good.

I won a chocolate raspberry ration packet off Teddy Johnson once. His Daddy had tha distribution store up in Perta and a stall in tha marketplace. He always gave Teddy specials. I bet Teddy a gaze and then went a whole seven minutes gazin down a mean wrinkled ole red feathered hen, one he said was too old ta pay 'tention. But at seven minutes Teddy made me laugh. But that was all right. He'd went first and only made it thirty seconds befoe she started bobbin her head and thumpin that firetail up and down. "See," he said. "That hen can hold 'tention." I was kinda famous fa that seven minutes. I coulda gone more, had befoe. I practiced all tha chances I got, like right then with little Bill and Jessy.

I hadn been timin mahself particular, but we must've been there a stretch, cuz I was startin ta wonder about it mahself.

And that's when I noticed it, high up there, right above Jessy's long purple plumes. First a shiny glint, and then, yep, there she was, in her full chromium splendor.

I identified tha class right off—a Warbler. Definitely. I could tell by tha two huge ball thruster engines stuck onta that even larger ball in tha middle. I had all tha rocket ship tradin cards. I even had a Warbler foil card. And that was a rare 'un. I got it off Teddy Johnson bettin I could jump higher than him. I was tha best jumper in tha third grade.

"Would'ya look at that," I said.

"What?" little Bill asked.

I clear stopped carin bout Jessy and spun mah tention down ta him, "I mean it. We got a visitor."

I grabbed little Bill by his shoulder and helped him up onta tha wall against tha chain link.

It was kinda funny cuz when he sprouted up, that ole lizard hen spooked, kicked-up red dirt—as we say Perta way—and shot out on a full sprint. Well, little Bill done spooked hisself an if I wasn holdn his shirt tight, he'd a flown clear back from that fence. "Sheesh," he said, soundin jess like Daddy.

"It's up there," I said, pullin mah own face right inta tha chain link. By that time there were already two cloudy pink chemtrails tailin out behind those round chroma side rockets.

"A Warbler," little Bill blurted. "Ya can tell by tha three bubbles."

I admit I probably did scrunch up mah face on account I woulda liked ta've said it first. But he was an is mah one and only little brother, so I jess said, "Why yes Bill, it is," like I hadn known.

And then we got ta whaddya expect.

"Who da ya think is comin way out here?" I asked. More ta mahself than ta him.

"Maybe they're off course," he answered jess tha same.

"Unlikely," I said.

"Well nobody evah lands out here. They're comin down from space."

And though little Bill was statin tha obvious, he was right. Nobody evah landed in our small town. Perta was a farm town. Ships came in an out of tha spaceports in New Vancouver an Covington, but most didn waste tha fuel ta git in an out of tha atmosphere. Tha Covington elevator up ta tha station was way cheaper. At least that's what everybody said. Sometimes tha older children would talk of tubes and spectrum travel, but Daddy nevah spoke of it, and neitha did anyone else, least not ta me.

So mah biggest wonder at tha time was why somebody would fly a ship all tha way out ta Perta ratha than jess drive a rover from tha city, or take tha hover, like everyone else?

"C'mon," I said. "We gotta tell Daddy tha news."

And whaddya expect, that's jess what we did. I helped mah brotha off tha wall, grabbed mah book bag, and we kicked-up red dirt down tha fence side road.

Mah run home would've been faster—I'm tha fastest runner in tha third grade—but I had mah little brotha ta think about. I held his hand tight in mine and made smaller steps so I could make quick ones. That's a trick I learned ta keep me in practice and make little Bill go faster, if ya can imagine that. I mean, if ya know little Bill today, he's over two meters high, but he wasn then. I recall mah mind racin at all of tha possibilities that Warbler and her crew coulda been bringin with her ta our small farm town. I'd nevah actually met anybody from outside of town befoe. Not even seen anybody really. There were traders who had stalls in tha Perta market, and they went back and forth ta tha cities, but that didn count cuz they were at tha market all tha time. And there was tha crowd at tha raceway each month, but that was tha same too. Little Bill's mind must've been racin too cuz he was shootin off questions as fast as he was runnin, so fast I doen know how he had a breath. "Ginny," he said, "Ya think there's a circus in there?"

"Too small," I said.

"Maybe jess an elephant?"

"Elephants are extinct."

"But not Syn elephants, they got one in Covington."

"Maybe," I said, and then we got ta whaddya expect, we started guessin there were space pirates inside, then ocean pirates. Little Bill said it could be tha demon like Maro, the one we'd seen in tha newsfeeds from Earth, or tha tentacle alien ancients tha older kids talked about, an on an on. Little Bill kept rattlin until I swear he listed all of tha characters tha Librarian read ta us from tha Archive. I answered mah duty, but I thought hard about mah Warbler tradin card. It said tha ship could hold seven, plus a cargo bay. That was too small fa a circus, but tha right size fa a family, an entire family. A whole family movin ta Perta all at once, and I thought, *Wouldn that be nice?* And maybe I'd have a friend too, somebody who'd been somewhere and done somethin, somebody that might invite me ta go places.

It was right then and there that Warbler soared above our heads, as if tha pilot were steerin by tha fence road itself.

Oh, tha excitement.

Little Bill was excited too. He was huffin and puffin at mah side as we rounded tha fence ta our house, a cloud of red dust trailin behind. I started yellin, "Daddy, Daddy." And little Bill echoed me. But Daddy didn answer.

Tha huge six-wheeled rover was in tha yard so I figured Daddy was in tha house.

Little Bill and I ran inta tha greenhouse fa coats-boots-hands—that's what Daddy calls it when we git home an we have'ta take off our coats, boots, an wash the red dirt off of our hands or else you-know-what. So we dropped on tha bench. I tore away tha Velcro straps along tha sides of mah boots, slipped mah feet out, and then helped little Bill cuz he was still strugglin with his. We left our book bags and jackets in a pile an scurried ta tha cistern ta rinse tha red dust from our hands—me maybe a bit more thoroughly than little Bill—and then we raced up tha glass corridor ta tha house ta tell Daddy tha excitin news.

I threw open tha door ta tha kitchen and froze still, only ta be bumped from little Bill as he ran inta mah backside.

Now there are sights ta be seen in yer life that yer mind takes a picture of and this here was one of 'em.

Seated at tha table, our table, was a stranger.

Daddy was with him, this man I'd nevah met, but, none tha less, there was a stranger at our table. Hardly anybody evah came ta our table. Cept ole Mrs. Tyler when she nosied around ta check in, always lookin fa company and free strawberries. Daddy said she was jess lonely since Mr. Tyler died. He was pegged in tha head by a race bird. Ya don git too close ta striders, that's a rule ta know.

I eyed tha stranger. He was strange all over. Fa one, he was jess too golden. His yellow hair was in perfect place—helmet hair, like tha men on tha news feeds—and his gray jacket and slacks were brand new, so smooth they didn look like they'd evah been worn, not even right then and there, while he had em on, and tha fabric of his cream colored shirt was so fine, not at all thick and heavy like every single piece of cloth on our farm. And tha boots he wore, oh tha surface of tha boots, so shiny, it was like tha reflection of tha table leg was right deep inside em.

And when I made mah eyes back up ta his face, he was smilin at me, an not jess any smile, but a real warm an kindly smile like little Bill's. I doen mean he smiled in that way little Bill smiles, all nice and cheery, cept I guess I do, but it was more than that. What I mean is he had tha same lookin smile. I'd been so busy taken in tha rest of 'em, I'd missed his face—he was familiar, not a stranger a'tall.

"Ginny," Daddy said, "Are ya gonna jess stand there with yer jaw hangin open or are ya gonna ta say hello ta yer Uncle Bill?"

I guess mah jaw was open. But whaddya expect seein a stranger at yer table. Now I know I jess said he weren no stranger, but that was on account of there hadn been no vistors cept' tha neighbor lady, and b'sides, I only saw tha familiar when I saw his face. I had nevah actually met mah Uncle Bill befoe. Until right then, he was jess a picture in tha sittin area I'd seen it so many times, I'd stopped lookin at it.

"You're not in yer uniform," I said.

"You're not in yer uniform," little Bill said behind me.

"I'm not in my what?" mah Uncle asked. His voice was as clean as his suit. Come ta think of it, mah Daddy's had suddenly gone smooth too, and would stay that way fa a time. Ya know it's funny what a child—maybe especially a girl child—nevah sees, or only wants ta see in her Daddy.

"Yer uniform," little Bill said. "Like yer picture. Ya wear yer uniform in tha picture."

Ma Uncle looked puzzled but mah Daddy cleared it up.

"Yer Homeland cadet uniform," Daddy said. "Little Bill here is referrin ta tha portrait we have hung up on tha wall in tha otha room. It's tha picture from officer trainin school, tha day of our graduation."

Uncle Bill nodded his head and returned that warm smile back ta us. Him jess lookin at us that way made me warm inside.

"Well, don't you both have great eyes," he said. "That picture was taken a long time ago."

"How come ya have tha same name as me?" little Bill asked.

"Cuz silly," I said. "Ya was named after Uncle Bill. This here is Mommy's brother."

"Ya knew mah Mommy," little Bill asked but befoe our Uncle could answer, anotha stranger entered tha kitchen. Now again I know you're gonna say that these people aren strangers if I know them, but fact is, I barely did. And though tha beautiful thin blonde woman enterin tha kitchen was surely mah Aunt Faye, with the bright white dress of fine lace she was wearin, an the way her golden hair flowed softly over her shoulders, she coulda been a fairie princess out of tha Archive. After seein nothin but red dust and our dull walls fa so long, I was practically numb, stunned by what that woman wore. I ain't nevah seen a finer thing. Mah Daddy and mah Uncle must've been taken too cuz it took a minute fa eitha of them ta say anythin, and even then only after mah Aunt Faye spoke first. And when she spoke, I admit I must've melted a bit inside, jess a little mind you. Sure, she had tha smooth talk like mah Uncle, but it was more than that, there was somethin in there that I heard befoe—but not since Mommy.

"Bill," she said. "Are you going to properly introduce me to these darling children?"

I remember that. She called us 'darling'. And of course Uncle Bill did, and that was how it came to be that we met our Aunt Faye. And that would be a story in itself. And I'd be happy with that. But what came next was an even better surprise: we were joined in tha kitchen by mah cousins Lilly and little Sal, and their Syn butler Sam.

It was jess as I had imagined. A whole family had come ta Perta. And even better than friends, they were mah family.

Daddy told us right off that things were goin ta be different. Uncle Bill and his family had come all tha way from Titan ta join us on Mars. All tha family I knew that were ta exist anywhere in all space were goin ta be right there in one place.

That sounded right ta me.

So there we were, at tha dinin table, havin our first meal all togetha as a family. It was me, little Bill, and Daddy—as always of course—but then there were four new faces, well, five if ya count Sam. Lilly and Sal were about tha same age as little Bill and me, so tha grownups put us at tha same end of tha table. Our cousins were full of interest and I spose we were as odd ta them as them ta us. They were askin whaddya expect, "Are there lots of children here to play with?" little Sal asked little Bill and, "What do you do for fun," Lilly asked me. But, as truly excited as I was, ta meet mah cousins, I have ta admit at that first meal I was a bit rude. I didn mean ta be. But as happy as I was ta've a new friend, I was drawn ta tha otha end of tha table. Ya see little Bill and I had seen otha children befoe. There weren a lot of them in Perta, not hundreds, but more than a few, enough ta fill tha school. Most of tha farmers were families come ta settle and I saw tha kids mah own age in tha third grade every day. What I weren used ta seein was a lady in tha way of mah Aunt Faye. Sittin at tha otha end of tha table, with tha window behind her, her yellow hair glowin gold, her eyes twinklin. Her cheeks were full and rosy and when she wasn laughin, she sounded like she was about ta. And so——fa once—did mah Daddy. His voice'd become all cheery and smooth, not in tha same way as mah Aunt an Uncle —they was mah Mommy's people—but he wasn talkin like a Perta farmer anymore. He spoke of higher things. He'd even gotten up befoe dinner and returned ta tha table with a jacket I'd nevah seen him wear that was about as fancy as Uncle Bill's but a few shades darker.

Little Bill was jess as caught up in tha Syn. We'd seen Syns in tha same way we'd seen women, all about town. But in tha same way I'd nevah met a lady like mah Aunt Faye, we'd nevah seen a Syn like Sam.

So ya might ask, what's so special about a Syn if you've seen one befoe? First off, he may have been a Syn, but he was handsome, caramel skin, thick coal-black curly hair, and of course tha too blue eyes all Syns have. Doen forgit neitha little Bill nor I had evah stepped foot off Mars. Had nevah ventured from Perta yet, fa that matter, and weren yet old enough ta know tha histories from tha Archive. Lookin back, that alone probably woulda made Sam even more special, cuz by tha time I was a girl, Syns like him were already long banned back on Alpha Earth.

But, like I said, we didn know tha full histories of tha Archive back then. We was too young. Tha only Syns we knew were tha workers. They were all about Perta, in tha huge greenhouses on tha west side of town, laborin fa tha merchants at tha markets, at tha Hover haulin pallets from tha rovers up onta tha platform and back, and tendin to the barns at the raceway. Even Teddy Johnson's daddy had two that worked fa him tween tha distribution store and tha storehouse out back. But all of those Syns wore thick canvas workmen's clothes and were quiet when they worked, keepin to themselves. They nevah said anythin ta ya, and if ya made it too close ta them, they would pick up and walk away jess not ta be yer bother.

Sam wasn at all like tha others. I think he knew it too. Sam dressed in clothes as fine as mah Aunt and Uncle, and he changed them regularly, sometimes several times a day. And he wasn quiet at all, he spoke, a lot, with an accent like Sir Alastair, tha man who ran tha raceway. And not jess when answerin a question. He asked a lot of questions, and he gave tha orders too. He'd tell Lilly and little Sal what ta do right up—and they had ta do it or else what. And he cooked, and he cleaned, he read Archive books ta mah cousins and I.

On that first day, we were jess impressed ta meet him.

But I'm gittin ahead of mahself.

Little Bill slapped me on mah arm and said softly, "Would ya look at that," and I turned ta mah right ta see Sam carryin two large trays, one in each hand, above his head from tha kitchen. He placed them in tha center of tha table. Tha fruits and vegetables sliced and arranged across tha face of tha platters were like an art piece. Daddy always kept us well fed, grains and supplements in tha mornin, meats and vegetables fa tha evenin main. But there was always a meat—we were farmers. I was bout ta ask jess where tha meat was, but mah Uncle spoke first, so I decided ta wait.

"What's it like farming dinosaurs?" he asked.

Mah Daddy didn miss a hitch. "Well," he said, "some people still like a lean wild tastin red meat that doesn come from a Syn creature," then he cocked a brow, all playful, like when he was bout ta school mah Uncle somethin, "and tha ornithomimids," those are tha lizard birds, of course, "produce a lot. Those striders are eighty percent hindquarters, not ta mention tha eggs."

"Tha eggs are as big as mah head," added Little Bill, and they were, and all of tha grownups laughed at that.

Daddy smiled our way and finished sayin, "Anyway, you'll find out soon enough. We *farm* tha produce, we *breed* and *raise* tha striders."

Ma Uncle raised a wedge of melon or pear maybe. He wasn convinced. "I'll do my best to do my part. But for dinner I'll stick to my greens, thank you."

"Ya know," Daddy said, "we breed a few of tha striders jess fa racing?"

Well I'da thought lightenin struck both mah Uncle and mah Aunt and I'm sure fa different reasons, cuz if Uncle Bill had no interest in Daddy's birds fa eatin, he'd suddenly developed a keen one fa somethin else. I mean both their eyes brightly lit up like tha fireworks on Settlers Day, Uncle Bill's toward Daddy and Aunt Faye's ta Uncle Bill.

"Really?" he asked. "These striders race?"

"Now don't be silly," Aunt Faye said across tha table ta Uncle Bill.

"Our Imperial is racin this Saturday," I said.

Mah Uncle turned his kind eyes right to me. "Tell me all about 'em," he said. And I did.

Our school was in Perta proppa, of course, and tha walk ta school was a good one. I liked it anyway. And I think it was excitin fa Lilly and little Sal jess tha same. Aunt Faye was insistin on Sam escortin us all ta school, so he did. I thought he would take away tha fun but he was jess as taken with all tha sights as Lilly and litte Sal.

That is, once we made our way inta Perta.

Even with all tha mountains surroundin, Perta sits under a mighty big sky. I spose walkin tha fence road ta git there was no glory for them. It hadn occurred ta me what'd been like growin up on Titan, livin below tha surface, under tha dome, and then travelin all that time over ta Mars in a Warbler. I noticed right off they kept their eyes down ta tha ground. Every few steps Lilly would veer inta me. "Excuse me," she'd say, sway back ta tha fence, and then repeat tha same thing again.

Little Sal was doin tha same.

Sam, of course, was walkin a straight line, but even he was tiltin his head ta tha road. I thought that strange, for a Syn.

But as soon as we made it ta Perta things picked up. I guess it was tha proximity of tha buildins, bein so close and cozy and all.

Like I said befoe, Perta is a small town, ya come over tha hill and there it is all in one glance.

Tha first things take yer eye are tha big glinty greenhouses over on tha side of town with tha rows of silos lined up next ta 'em. Daddy says there was a time, back when people still lived inside, that all of tha food fa our town was grown in those glass buildins. Now they jess do tha big crops in there. Tha rest of tha town doen look like much till ya git close, cubes and boxes I spose. But once yer in tha town it livens right up. Perta is laid out like a grid so there's no way ya can git lost. Tha dirt road that leads ta Daddy's farm joins a bunch of others at that hill there on tha edge of town, and as soon as we stepped foot over it we saw otha children headin in and a lot more people movin about. I think that made things easier too.

Tha boys started kickin about, as boys do, and it wasn till we came close ta tha Hover platform that little Sal stopped in his tracks.

"What's that?" he asked.

"Ain ya nevah seen no Hover befoe?" little Bill asked back.

I shushed him and Sam said, "That, young sir, is a train. It is a networked transportation system utilized for hauling goods and people."

We watched everyone movin around the platform. People boarded the Hover on one side of the platform while on the other Syn workers in sunflower yella coveralls loaded and unloaded cargo destined fa cities and places I doen know.

I saw that Lilly was lookin very serious, and then she said, "It's a tube. An above ground tube like back on Titan."

"Why, yes," Sam said. "In a matter of speaking, it is."

I'd heard of tha tubes that ran through center of tha Earth between tha Bubble stations and I'd even heard of tubes that ran through space. Tha older children spoke of them. I wanted ta ask Lilly if that's what she was talkin bout. But I didn. I couldn. I had a hard time askin bout things I didn understand too much back then, guess I still do. I like ta find them out first.

When we was through dawdlin by tha platform, we moved on ta tha square in tha center of town. I pointed out whaddya expect, where tha distribution store was, tha market, course ya couldn miss Perta Town Hall, and finally tha playground and tha school. Little Bill and Sal kicked red dirt fa tha playground right off, they had time. Lee Lin and Millie Clawson, two friends of mine from tha third grade, was comin along tha walk.

"Tha last thing ya need," I told Lilly, "is ta've tha whole of tha third grade see ya bein walked ta school by yer parents' helper."

Lilly didn need no explainin and I was glad of that too. We were catchin on right fast.

"Sam," she said. "We're fine now."

"Very well, young miss," he said in that smooth and funny way. But that was about it. He made his way and we made ours till tha school day ended.

I had a wonderful day in school. I introduced mah cousin ta all of Ms. Tilly's class and felt so proud when Ms. Tilly told everyone she was from Titan. No one else in class had a cousin from Titan, in fact no one else in Ms. Tilly's class had evah been anywhere really or had anyone visit, ceptin Teddy Johnson, and maybe a few more that had been ta Covington, or somewhere, but fa sho none had family move in from Titan. We did tha Homeland pledge togetha and I showed Lilly where we were at in studies. We had lunch in tha arboretum under a tree and ate apple swans that Sam had carved fa us. An then, we sat quietly next ta each otha in science waitin fa one of Ms. Tilly's cocoons ta let loose a butterfly, and it did. And that's a story in itself.

I had tha best day with mah new special friend.

After school Sam was waitin fa us in tha square. I was so excited I forgot mah book bag inside and had ta run back ta git it. When I came back ta tha square that girl Helen was jess leaving. I expected somethin by Lilly's long face and tha way both Bill and Sal were pushin their boots forward inta tha red dust. That Helen couldn be happy unless she was makin trouble.

No care fer her, I mustered anyway.

"I have somethin super special ta show ya," I said. "Wait till ya see this. C'mon."

"I think we should go directly home," Lilly said. "Mother will be waiting."

I spose tha first day in a new school is tough fa anybody, but that Helen went and done somethin fer sure.

"What she say?" I asked in a huff.

"Nothing at all," Lilly said.

"Not true," little Bill said. "Helen done asked Sal why he talked funny."

I threw mah hands ta knees and leaned inta little Sal, "Is that so?"

"Yes," he said.

"Well. Doen mind her none. She's jealous."

"Why?"

"Two reasons. One, I'm fraid ta tell ya, but yer tha only one round here that knows how ta speak at all. And two, she probably figured I was about ta tell ya we're headin ta tha raceway ta see Daddy's Imperial and tha otha striders they have out there. Now ya sure ya gotta run home and ain gotta an extra minute?"

And that fixed that, cuz Sal and Lilly both chipped up. "I think we have time," Lilly said.

And that was good cuz I had already made up mah mind as ta what we were goin ta do and ta tha raceway we went with a skip our step.

Now tha raceway was on tha opposite side of Perta from where we came in, but our town is so small it only takes a few minutes ta git there. Ya jess go ta tha far edge and it's over tha next hill. I spose from tha air you'd see tha hill is really one big circle rim cuz Perta was built in a crater, but ya know I doen think I really knew that until I was much older.

When we hit tha top of tha hill, Lilly threw her hand over her face. "Oh my," she said, jess like a little lady.

"What's that smell?" little Sal asked.

"That's guano," little Bill said. "It's tha strider's—"

"Little Bill," I interrupted, unsure jess what he was about ta say. "Let's jess keep movin. It only smells right here cuz there's a breeze blowin from tha waste shed. We want ta go over ta tha big barns over there past the grandstands."

I pointed ta tha two barns over ta tha right of tha tall pink walled buildin in front of us. When we got around ta tha side, I would show mah cousins that tha big buildin was tha grandstands, an not the big flat it looked like from tha ridge of tha hill.

When we rounded down ta tha barns, we saw why tha smell was extra rosy. There were four Syns shovelin guano inta tha back bin of a small utility rover. I'm used ta a little odor—what daddy calls tha smell of money—but even I shielded mah face till we passed 'em, and once we were downwind clear, it weren so bad.

And if that nasty odor was a turn off then what came next made up fa it, cuz when Lilly and Sal saw that corner pen full of mini-striders, everyone was happy.

Now when I say mini, keep in mind we're still talkin bout striders, so even though tha pen was full of tha cutest spotted little fuzzballs ya evah did see, they still came up ta yer knees. Those were jess baby lizard birds and true enough they were nevah goin ta be as high as an Imperial, jess tha same, they were still goin ta be as tall as mah daddy, easy. But they were cute in tha kiddie pen and that's why I wanted ta take mah new special friend there ta see them. We cranked handfuls of feed pellets out of tha post mounted dispensers and let them lick right out of our hands.

Oh did little Bill and Sal giggle so and I spose Lilly and I did as well.

Things were peachy fine.

I'd near forgotten Sam was behind us until I heard him exlaim in that proppa voice of his, "Children, children, you must step down immediately." On account we were all climbin up on tha first rung of tha fence and leanin over instead of puttin our hands through.

"Doen worry," little Bill said. "We woen fall in. Sides, these striders are cuddly."

I done thought that Sam's too blue eyes were goin ta pop right out tha front of his face. I doen know which was more fun, those soft beak tickles or tauntin poor old Sam. Anyway, we'd had enough of tha giggles and I could see that poor Syn needed a rest so I said, "Lets' go see Blue," and tha otha three children followed right behind. Blue, of course, was mah Daddy's strider and we'd find 'em on tha otha side of tha barn in tha trainin pens where tha bigger birds was stretched out.

Since tha Syns was cleanin tha inside of tha strider barn, we walked tha outside. Each pen, like tha kiddie pen, had a door that led back inta tha stables, but most all of tha lizards were out fa tha air. These were tha smaller ones, of course, tha big brothers of tha fuzzball minis in tha kiddie pen, but they were jess as glorious ta look at as their tall cousins out back and little Bill was listin them off like ole Sir Alastair himself—but without tha funny accent.

"That there's a true Platy," he said, pointin ta tha black-headed silver bird. "That's short fa Platinen."

"Platinum," I corrected.

"And that one next ta it too?" Sal asked, noddin ta tha same size bird in tha next pen.

"No," mah brotha said. "That's an Ash. See, he's all one color. Tha Platy's head and neck is black. That next one is a short bill, and this one here's a spotted."

Lilly stopped in front of tha next pen. "Who is this beautiful creature, little Bill?"

"I doen know his name," little Bill said, "but he's a bearded strider."

I tapped a small plate on his pen and said, "It's Chilton," softly though, not ta upset Bill fa not bein able ta read. I could see by tha way he was side eyein me that he was already short with me fa correctin 'em tha first time.

Lilly's head tilted ta tha side as if she were tryin ta find a way ta take in more than she could. "He has a pink beak and crest and all of his plumage is grass green. He is so," she paused and scrunched up her face. I could tell she was searchin fa jess tha right word. And then she said it. "Brilliant."

"Brilliant?" I repeated. "Ya know they're pretty, but they ain so smart."

"No. I mean the way the colors dance across the green of his pelt, and his beard is so," she stopped there and I waited fa tha next word, then she said it, "regal."

Let me tell ya I was soon to learn that mah cousin Lilly loved words.

"Oh yeah. Chilton here is a prince," I said. "But wait till ya see Blue. C'mon now."

And then tha walk went on as whaddya expect, cuz ole Chilton was tha first of a dozen striders that weren no more than show birds. Doen git me wrong. They was beautiful, tha rainbow crested Kulati, tha forest brown Remi, all in all, they're truly gentlemen breeds as mah Daddy would say, but they doen run, and they were'nt Blue, so not much interest ta me. Well it took a while to git Lilly down tha line. But that was okay with me cuz that was what we were there fa anyhow.

When we finally did round tha barns, I confess even I was taken. Iffen ya nevah seen a truly big bird up close, it'll stop yer heart. It's not like in tha picture books, those are jess, well, pictures. Hens is somethin ta see, three meters high, but a male is anotha meter easy, and tha males, jess like tha small lizards, are tha true dandies. They have all tha high crest colored combs and plumes fa prancin around, so that can add a whole otha meter. Ya can say that extra meter is jess fluff, but I doen think that matters much when ya have angry firetail sky towerin over ya.

And that's exactly what happened when we rounded that barn.

He wasn out in tha open. We wouldna been allowed that way if that was tha case. He was in a high chain link pen. But he was high over our heads in full glory, those bright red feathers flarin wide from his foe-arms, those orange and red plumes crownin his hard hissin head. Yadda thought there was a buildin wall of red feathers collapsin down on ya if ya were in mah place and that's what it was like.

I stepped back quick, so did Lilly, and Sal, and little Bill, I even heard Sam say, "Oh dear." But then I saw tha trainer on tha catwalk up above us in his raceway coveralls.

"It's alright," I said in a near hoarse voice. "The Demon's mad at him, not us."

"The Demon?" Lilly asked.

"That's his name," little Bill said.

"Why do they call 'em that?"

"Cuz he's a mean ole bird," said Bill. "What would ya call 'em?"

Everyone had their footin now and we'd spotted tha otha two trainers across tha catwalks on tha back and side.

"I doen know," Lilly said. "If he's so mean, why do they allow him to be here?"

"He's a large ornery bird," I said. "But he's a fast large ornery bird."

"He's a favorite most times," little Bill added. I doen think he knew what that meant, but he heard Daddy say it, so that was good enough.

Ole Demon took ta joltin his head forward and back and struttin across his space. And even though he paid no mind ta us, I still started a bit whenevah tha long bushy red tail would swoosh along to tha side. It was somethin to watch, tha two trainers from tha upper sides tryin ta harness him while tha one above us was ta pull tha birds attention.

Things were calmin down and we were jess about to move on when—I doen rightly know how it happened— one of tha trainers from tha back was off tha catwalk and on his way inta tha pen. I mean ta say he was hangin by his fingers, almost fell full in.

Well we all gasped hard cuz there was nuthin we could do, and right there in front of us that firetail threw up his full crown again and lashed forward.

It coulda been a horror on that day, but I'm glad to say it wasn.

Cuz jess then tha air filled with a "Chirp, chirp, chirp," and then anotha, "chirp, chirp, chirp." And ole Demon kicked red dirt, spun around toward tha barn, and who'da ya think we saw but his rider Bruto, armored head to toe in blood leather. Bruto used tha birdcall to distract that red giant and tha otha trainers pulled that man off tha chain link and away jess in time and, I guarantee, saved his life.

I give it ta Lilly and Sal cuz they didn go all wishy.

In fact, Lilly said, "I thought they were herbivores." All plainly like she was watchin a vid from tha Archive.

"Herbivore or not, that there firetail is mean. But that doen matter," I said. "We can pet tha striders in tha kiddie pens but tha rest are off limits. They'll attack a man and can kill 'em, easy, jess like that, jess cuz they're spooked."

"Ya doen git too close ta striders," little Bill chimed, "that's a rule ta know."

"But what about that man in red?"

"That's no ordinary man," I said. "That's tha bird's rider. Tha lizards imprint on tha riders right out of tha egg."

"He ain no man no how," little Bill said. "Helen says he's a Maro."

And as if tha Bruto could hear us from up near tha top of tha barn he turned his masked face toward us.

I gave little Bill a wink. "That's silly," I said, wonderin mahself if it were true, if Bruto was one of tha red eyed horned folk from tha Earth Planes that Daddy and Uncle Bill fought when they were soldiers. "I think we best be goin to see Blue now." And we were off.

Now Lilly had called that bearded bird with tha pink bill regal, and whaddya expect, she went on ta say tha same fa jess about every fancy feathered lizard she saw down that line of pens and out in tha big yard behind the barns. But there's only one breed that owns that title proppa, and those are tha Imperial striders. Mah Daddy's bred Imperials on his farm, like that hen Jessy I was tellin ya about befoe. Ole Blue, ya bet, was an Imperial too, and if ya thought that feisty Demon was tall, well, he was an easy head shorter than Blue, an that was befoe crest and crown. I was waitin to say as much to mah cousin and new special friend Lilly but when she saw him standin tall proppa with his rider beside him in his pen, why, she said so herself.

She lifted her chin straight up at that magnificent blue and purple strider and said, "Oh my, why you're king of them all."

And I was quite proud cuz I surely thought he was a king of tha striders if there evah was one, and he couldn have looked better right then with Mar's butter sunlight bringin out tha best in his color. "Lilly, Sal, may I introduce Blue and his rider, Mercer?"

"Look how he holds his head high while his rider strokes his neck and back," Sal said. "He doesn't even move. Not a flinch. Are you sure that's his rider?"

"Of course," little Bill said, "that's Mercer."

"Then why is he only wearin blue coveralls and not body armor like that otha rider was?"

"Cuz tha otha one's not human. Helen told me so. He's a Maro."

"What's a Maro?"

"She says they're red eyed, horned creatures from one of tha Earth planes."

"Cut that," I said, my eyes stern so he'd know I was serious. "Daddy says Bruto has to wear tha same thing all tha time cuz his strider imprinted him with it on and is too dumb to recognize him otherwise. That's all it is, Demon's dumb as a moon rock."

I wasn sure if that was true but it was jess then that Mercer took notice of us an I was glad of that. "Hi Ginny, little Bill, who is that there with ya?"

"Mercer, meet my cousins Lilly and little Sal. They've come all tha way from Titan to live here in Perta."

"Hello cousins Lilly and little Sal all tha way from Titan. I heard ya were comin. How'd ya like ta help me out today?"

"Sure," Lilly said.

"Great. Then can you and yer cousin go gatha a bucket of warm water from tha tack barn while yer brotha and Sal check my work?"

And off we went.

I always liked that Mercer was like that. There were a lot of nice riders at tha raceway, but they nevah really paid ya no mind, they'd smile and nod and be proppa polite, ceptin tha likes of Bruto of course, but fa tha most part they was dedicated to their steeds. Mercer was dedicated too—he rarely left Blue's side—but he still took tha time out fa sincere kindness. Maybe that was why Blue was such an honorable lizard, cuz of Mercer's influence. Most riders nevah have more than two steeds their there lives, some three, some only one, and I think that Blue was as proud of that twinkle eyed blonde haired man as he was of himself.

We went over to tha tack barn, Lilly and I, and we gathered tha bucket from Blue's room. I'd helped out plenty befoe so I was able to show Lilly what to grab. A bucket meant we were to also bring back tha big sponges. Once Mercer had wiped away tha loose red dust, he would give Blue a bath with a warm sponge. It was somethin to watch cuz good luck tryin to pin down a lizard bird with somethin wet if they were not wantin it themselves. But Mercer was able to take care of Blue like a baby brother.

All was goin peachy fine until we got to tha end of tha tack barn. That's where tha spigot is that ya use ta fill tha bucket. Cuz that's when I saw there were three men over at tha end of one of tha otha sheds and one of 'em sure looked like Uncle Bill.

"Isn that yer Daddy?" I asked.

"Yes," Lilly said. "We should go say hello."

I put my hand out in front of her and slid us both back behind tha corner of tha tack barn.

"I recognize those two men he's talkin to. Daddy say were spose to stay away from 'em. I think we better stay outta site."

"Who are they?"

"They work fa Mister Black Hat."

"That's a funny name."

"That's not his real name. That's jess what we call 'em. His real name's Brewster. He owns tha roadhouse up tha way."

"What's a roadhouse?"

"I doen know fa sure. But grownups go there and drink too much wine. Daddy said that tha roadhouse and Mister Black Hat and all his men are trouble."

"What do you suppose those men are writing down?"

"Doen know that either. But we better go fetch water from tha otha end."

And that's what we did.

Lilly didn say anythin as we filled tha bucket. She didn say anythin until we were almost back to Blue's pen. And then she said, "Ginny?"

"Yeah," I said.

"Could you not say anything about seeing my Daddy by the raceway today? Cuz I don't want to have to leave Perta the way we left Titan."

I kept mah promise true and didn say a word about seein my cousin's daddy at the raceway and that was the best cuz things were peachy fine up to tha day of tha race. What an excitin day it was. Ya haven felt true excitement if ya nevah seen striders race.

Tha day of tha race I was high up in tha stands overlookin tha raceway with Little Bill and my cousins. By tha time tha smaller striders finished up two races, little Bill was already complainin his belly was aching. We had all kinds of specials, on account that Blue was racin, and on account that Lilly and little Sal had nevah been to a race. We'd eaten frozen pops, jelly candy, and Sal even tried a meaty syn stick. I think he loved it, even though

Aunt Faye didn approve. Lilly wouldn try one but that was her loss.

Chilton, tha bearded strider that Lilly adored so, was in tha winner's circle in front of tha stands. Receivin his accolades fa winnin tha quarter K run. Tha dozen or so fancy feathered midsized birds that'd trailed ta tha finish behind 'em were gathered down ta tha left side so that tha trainers could remove tha little mechanical jockeys from their backs. But what everyone was really focused on was what was happenin on tha right side or in tha stands. Tha eight K race was about to begin and tha riders were filin their tall mounts inta tha pit behind tha startin gate.

Tha crowd was mixed inta hurrahs and awes, some callin out who they was rootin fo. When that mean ole Demon came around tha corner, almost tha whole grandstand yelled, "Boo," and, "Red devil." A bald man near tha edge threw somethin over tha side, I think his meat stick, an that bird cranked his head up at tha crowd with jolt and let out a menacin hiss. I was clear across tha stands and I jumped back, shirked mah shoulders and all. We all did. That firetail may have been a favorite ta win, but he wasn anybody's favorite any otha way.

It was a whole otha story when Mercer brought Blue out, "Look Mommy," little Sal yelled. "There's Blue." He was tha first of us to see 'em, but people young and old across tha stands had already started chantin his name. "Blue, Blue, Blue," they all said at once, and we joined in too, until Blue stopped jess befoe tha pit and set eyes up at that huge crowd, and both he and Mercer bowed their heads. Whaddya expect, tha whole entire grandstand broke out inta a frenzy right then and I doen blame a single one of them a bit.

Aunt Faye was on her feet with everyone else, her twinklin eyes alight. I could tell that most of tha day she was playin along, but now she seemed to be havin real fun. "Your strider appears to have a great amount of popularity," she said to mah Daddy. "He must be a real winner."

"That's not it," I said.

"Oh no?"

"See, Blue isn jess popular cuz he wins so much. I mean he does win a lot, but not all tha time. Fact is, some of tha birds a bit smaller than him can jess plain out maneuver and out run 'em, so it's not cuz he wins. Blue's popular cuz he's truly majestic. Besides, ya not allowed ta wager none so ya have ta root fa tha good."

My Aunt always smiles but her cheeks went full in that special way when I said that.

"What are they doing now Ginny? The riders are reaching around to the muzzles. Are they feeding the striders?"

"Yeah. Right now they're givin 'em fruit. It's a tradition at tha gate. See how they're whisperin in tha striders ears?"

"Oh yes. I didn't realize they all were doing that."

"That means tha race is about to start."

An on cue, Sir Alastair's surly accent echoed through tha sound system. "Ladies and Gentlemen," and on he went with his high praise and introduction of each strider, an there were more cheers and more boos and whaddya expect, tha klaxon sounded with a deafenin squak. Tha sound pinched mah ears in such a way I had to throw mah hands up. But my eyes were glued on that rainbow assortment of birds burstin away and down tha track.

What's happening?" Lilly asked. "What are all of those machines flying next to the track?"

"Those are tha drones," I said. I pointed up at tha huge panels high above tha grandstands, at a runnin side view of the pack across tha screens. "Thay're capturin tha video." Then I jerked mah neck back toward Daddy. Lilly looked at him and then back ta me and we giggled cuz, with tha race in front of 'em and tha huge screen above, whaddya expect, Daddy was focused on a screen in his hand. Uncle Bill was jess tha same.

"Your Daddy's funny," Lilly said.

"He's jess watchin that cuz it's from tha drone focused on Blue."

"Oh." She squinted out toward tha end of tha track. "How far do they go?"

"Eight kilometers. So they'll go four klicks out and then back."

"It looks like they're floating on ripples."

"That's a fata morgana," Sam said.

"A what?" I asked.

"A mirage."

I'd never heard it called that but they was referrin to tha way tha dust causes an illusion at tha far end of tha track.

Soon tha striders were out of sight and we looked to tha screen above.

"Who's the lemon yellow strider in the lead?" Aunt Faye asked.

Little Bill was quick to answer, "That's Faron, he woen win."

"He won't?" Aunt Faye's bow scrunched togetha in a funny way.

I could tell she was tryin to make sense of it all but was strugglin.

"What little Bill means," Daddy said, "is that he's one of tha fastest sprinters, but he doesn have tha stamina ta hold tha lead past four k."

"Oh," Aunt Faye said.

And it went on like whaddya expect fa tha next fifteen minutes. Faron fell away and Vanu stole tha lead, Blue and Demon jostled fa position, there were brief starts and fits until tha crowd began to rumble and little Bill said, "There they are."

Sho enough, a random kaleidoscope of colors were floatin far on tha red dust horizon. Tha dozen shimmerin figures seemed separate and unrelated ta tha digitally clear images on tha huge screens above our heads.

I must've stopped breathin cuz when I went to speak, no words came out. I gulped some air and said, "I see Blue." And I did. That giant lizard may've been almost horizontal in full run. A dark blue bird usually ain no more than a mere dark dot. But I saw him clear as day.

"They're comin in fast," I said.

"They sure are," Lilly said.

People began ta push forward from tha top of tha stands down and those on tha sides were pressed ta tha railings.

Tha large screen above focused on one strider, Blue.

"Blue's winning," yelled Sal.

Tha crowd stomped their feet tha way they do and tha entire stand roared and rumbled in a thunda. I felt my insides jumpin—tha way they always do—my cousins and even my Aunt Faye was tha same.

Then tha image pulled back and anotha face crept onto tha screen. It was that evil lizard Demon. An he wasn jess movin up, he was cruzin by ole Blue with eaze until, if jess by a nose, he was in tha lead.

Ya couldn hear yer own thoughts right then if ya wanted ta. Tha crowd was crazy. This was tha best loved and tha most hated, right there together, both tha birds neck forward, feathers back, and tha little clock in tha corner read sixty-five k, can ya believe sixty-five. They was runnin a track record.

It was right then that Blue got somethin in em an eazed his nose up to tha front.

Tha crowd nevah went quiet befoe, not toward tha end of a race. But they did right then. They went from hootin and booin and stompin to nothin. Every one there in tha stands, all of Perta whaddya expect, stopped even a breath.

Now if ya were out there on tha track, ya wouldn be able to tell which of those flyin striders was in tha lead and ya sure couldn tell from way up high in tha stands, but those drones all worked togetha to create an exact picture and what was on tha big screen weren't no lie. An maybe it was tha blessin of tha Imperials extra length, that head long that tha firetail jess didn have, cuz even though thay was stride fa stride in that last quarter k up to tha finish line, it was ole Blue's head that came across first.

An ya shouldda heard tha yellin that day.

After tha big race I was both exhausted an full of life all at once. So was mah new best friend Lilly. She was practically jumpin up an down, but then so was Sal, and so was Aunt Faye, if ya can believe it. She had a lace handkerchief in hand and was dabbin her forehead as a lady does.

"This happens every week?" mah Aunt asked mah Daddy.

"Yes," he said so proud.

"That's so exciting," she went on, "and no wagering?"

"No. It's not allowed."

I'm not sure my Aunt believed him cuz then she asked, "Then how can little Perta afford all of this?"

But mah Daddy was quick to assure her, "It's streamed ta the cities fa entertainment."

"I see. It's a lot to take in."

"Well, we do this, but tha rest of tha day we'll spend at tha market."

I'm not sure why she was so concerned after havin such a wonderful time but she musta liked what Daddy said cuz her face went pleasant.

To be sure, I added, "Since Blue won we'll git a bonus to take to tha market."

"Oh. I see," she said, an then that was okay.

Daddy was gatherin his things. "I better git down to the winner's circle with Mercer. Would anyone like to come?"

An whaddya expect mah cousins did a dance an we were on our way.

~*~

We pooled togetha tha big new family an filed down tha steps with all of tha crowd.

"Isn't anybody going to wait to see Blue receive his prize?" Lilly asked, as we waited ta move through tha queue.

"Naw," I said. "Tha winner's circle is fa Blue, Mercer, and tha vids."

"So they'll be watching us in the cities?"

"Oh yeah. I spose. Nevah thought of it," I said and I hadn up till then.

"If that's the case," Uncle Bill said. "I think I'll head over to the snack bar."

"Oh Bill," Aunt Faye said, "we're going to the market right after."

"I know. But I'm thirsty from the dust and yelling and, to be honest, I'm not quite ready for the vids." My uncle let a sweet smile creep slowly onta his face that was jess so cute an charmin. So of course, Aunt Faye said, "All right. You go ahead. We'll catch up with you." An off he went. Whaddya expect he was jess two meters away when little Sal said, "I wanna go with Daddy." An little Bill chimed in, "Me too." And Aunt Faye said okay an they scuttled behind, surely wantin more of those meat sticks in tha bread, but they jess didn say.

An all went fine. We went to tha winners circle an there was Blue all tall and proud, Mercer standin next to 'em. Course no one else was really allowed close, even fa a fine behaved bird like Blue. We all had to stand outside tha circle. But if ya saw tha image we was made to look like we was standin closer, like right beside tha family treasure that big Imperial was.

This wasn tha first time by no means that Blue had won, but it was still a pleasure and it was a first fa Lilly an Aunt Faye. I think both of them enjoyed havin their picture taken an I found mahself doin what they did, standin taller, straightenin mah back, puttin mah right leg out in front of mah left, jess a little. They were friendly to tha vids and tha vids were friendly to them. We were havin so much fun, we were forgittin about Daddy takin care of business an wherevah Uncle Bill an tha boys went. I guess it dawned on Aunt Faye, cuz she said, "Ginny and Lilly, why doen you two round up your brothers. It's almost time to go."

An that's what we set out ta do.

Ceptin when we found them, they was runnin to find us.

Little Bill may've been only five years old at the time but even then he could find his way jess about anywhere. I'm not sayin he had tha outright sense ta map ya from tha market ta mah Daddy's farm. I'm jess sayin that if he'd been somewhere, like tha raceway, he wasn lost. An good thing cuz Sal woulda been had.

When we didn find them by tha snack bar we thought fa sure they'd be over by tha pens lookin at tha striders. When Lilly an I saw them runnin toward us from tha barns, I could tell straight away there was trouble.

Both tha boys were huffin, an though little Bill was tryin ta git some words out, his breath was cheatin 'em.

"Calm down, calm down," I said. "What's wrong? Where's Uncle Bill?"

An while I was askin that to little Bill, Lilly was doin tha same with Sal.

"It's tha Black Hat's men," Little Bill said. "They have 'em."

I wasn sure what ta do but I had ta think quick. There weren't no grownups near tha barns, no Syns neither. Everyone was still by tha stands or on tha way back ta tha market square.

"Lilly," I said. "Go git mah Daddy. I'll see what's happenin here."

An off she ran, one way with tha boys, an I ran tha other. I had a sense where ta go. I jess kinda knew, bad bein bad, and mean bein mean. I went right ta Demon's pen. An sure enough, right when I got there in sight, I saw those same two thugs that Uncle Bill had been talkin ta tha otha day, dangling em from tha catwalk. And befoe I could say boo they threw em from tha catwalk inta tha firetail's pen.

I looked up at them, but they paid me no mind. They jess walked their way to leave my Uncle in there alone with that mean ole Demon, an that firetail lizard surely had taken notice.

Maybe that ornery red bird was extra angry foe losin that race, or cuz Bruto hadn stuck around to soothe him down, which in itself shouldda made me wonder, but no matter what, that lizard bird was madder than usual and went right ta tauntin mah Uncle by jeerin side to side and pivotin his neck back an forth in quick jolts, like he was gonna strike, but not.

Ma Uncle made it ta his feet. He had his arms out ta his sides and his legs wide, ready ta dart eitha way. But ya have ta think, that strider was three times his height. Demon came down close to Uncle Bill's head with a lightnin strike and then, jess missin 'em, recoiled. Mah uncle dove outta tha way, but if Demon wanted ta hit 'em, he would've.

Then I heard a "Chirp, chirp, chirp," and it wasn comin from no Bruto or any otha strider whistle. It was comin from me.

That firetail locked eyes on me and whaddya expect? I did what I was sposed to, I locked back.

Now Helen wasn the only that said the birds can git inta yer mind, fry yer pan. Teddy Johnson said so too. So did lots of folks. An I doen know about whetha that's true or not. At that point in my life I'd gazed inta the eyes of plenty roosters an hens alike and woulda said not, but I nevah gazed inta tha swellin heated eyes of a strider tha likes of that firetail Demon. An if ya believe that an animal, a mean animal, can have somethin in it that shouldn be there, some kinda evil, or hate, that ole bird had it. I could see straight through, deep inta whatevah that evil was. I was seein probably more than a young girl should see. But that day it was best I did, and was best it was me, cuz that bird was strong, gazin back, and if there was any truth to a lizard fryin a pan then he'd be tha one to do it.

Tha longer I peered inta spiralin twisted abyss of that birds soul, tha more I fought to keep control. I fought until tha barns around me were no more, and tha pen around me had disappeared, until even mah Uncle an tha long bushy orange tale of tha beast had faded out an away. I fought until it was me an that strider, somewhere else, on one of those planes, like back on Earth.

An then I realized that ole Demon, was fightin too. Demon was fightin real hard, harder than me, but not hard enough. An it was jess like that tha world came back, an I saw him frozen stiff, under mah spell, an I saw his huge crest rest back, an his long red-orange bushy tale fall to tha red dirt. I saw tha men from town were pullin Uncle Bill outta that pen.

I heard my Daddy say "Sheesh," in that way that he useta.

It wasn said to us, but Lilly and I picked up quick Uncle Bill had made a wager with Black Hat's men. He had to git sorted with Aunt Faye, and that took some time, but after that, we was all one peachy fine happy family.

An me? Daddy said he saw then that I was a natural and told me that one day I could match with an egg if I wanted, become a rider. But that's anotha story—and it all started with gazin.

They call it gazin, tha way ya lock eyes on one of tha lizard birds, make 'em freeze solid, stare back inta yours. I was really good at it, say so mahself. Best in Ms. Tilly's third grade fa sure, best on Mars maybe, ceptin Daddy of course.

~*~

ABOUT THE AUTHORS

Jessica West (a.k.a. West1Jess) is currently pursuing a state of self-induced psychosis, also known as writing. In the past, she has worked for Wal-Mart, a lawyer, and a bank. Now if she could just get a couple years experience with the IRS and the NSA, world domination is in the bag.
Jess lives in Acadiana with three daughters still young enough to think she's cool and a husband who knows better but likes her anyway.

For more information, visit west1jess.com

Daniel Arthur Smith is a USA Today bestselling author. His titles include *Spectral Shift*, *Hugh Howey Lives, The Cathari Treasure, The Somali Deception*, and a few other novels and short stories. He also curates the phenomenal short fiction series *Tales from the Canyons of the Damned*.

He was raised in Michigan and graduated from Western Michigan University where he studied philosophy, with focus on cognitive science, meta-physics, and comparative religion. He began his career as a bartender, barista, poetry house proprietor, teacher, and then became a technologist and futurist for the Fortune 100 across the Americas and Europe.

Daniel has traveled to over 300 cities in 22 countries, residing in Los Angeles, Kalamazoo, Prague, Crete, and now writes in Manhattan where he lives with his wife and young sons.

For more information, visit danielarthursmith.com

~*~